PIRATE Chicken
ALL HENS ON DECK

WORDS BY BRIAN YANISH
PICTURES BY JESS PAUWELS

sourcebooks
jabberwocky

FOR **A.D.**, WHO TAUGHT ME TO FOLLOW MY CREATIVE JOURNEYS WHEREVER THEY LEAD. —**B.Y.**

TO ALL THE GIRLS LIVING THEIR DREAMS. —**J.P.**

Text copyright © 2019 by Brian Yanish
Illustrations copyright © 2019 by Jess Pauwels
Cover and internal design © 2019 by Sourcebooks, Inc.

Sourcebooks and the colophon are registered trademarks of Sourcebooks, Inc.

The art was first sketched in pencil, then rendered in color using digital techniques.

Published by Sourcebooks Jabberwocky, an imprint of Sourcebooks, Inc.
P.O. Box 4410, Naperville, Illinois 60567–4410
(630) 961-3900
Fax: (630) 961-2168
sourcebooks.com

Library of Congress Cataloging-in-Publication Data is on file with the publisher.

Source of Production: Shenzhen Wing King Tong Paper Products Co. Ltd., Shenzhen, Guangdong Province, China
Date of Production: December 2018
Run Number: 5013626

Printed and bound in China.
WKT 10 9 8 7 6 5 4 3 2 1

Lily was not an ordinary chicken.

While other chickens pecked, she plotted.

They roosted. She read.

They were happy to live life on the farm.

But Lily wanted to see
The World. She knew
she was meant for more.

So by chance, when a band of pirates invaded one day,
Lily saw her moment.

"I'm scared," clucked one hen.

"I'm going to hide in my nest," squawked another.

The pirates gathered up all the chickens
and took them to their ship.

At sea, Lily was
a fast learner.

Where's the
poop deck?

But the pirates paid no attention
to a silly chicken.

One afternoon they stopped at an island, and the pirates forgot one very important thing.

While the pirates sang and danced the night away, the ship drifted.

And by morning, the chickens were in charge.
Lily had, of course, prepared for this.

Her loud voice boomed across the deck of the ship.

ALL HENS ON DECK!

The chickens clucked to attention.

Lily taught the hens to read the maps,

hoist the sails,

and steer the ship.

They sailed to fantastic new lands,

they sang the rowdiest sea songs,
and held the most outrageous chicken dances!

But Lily still
wanted more.

She rounded up the crew one day.

The chicken crew looked at her blankly.

"HOORAY!"

Before long, Lily was known by a different name.

Redfoot ate the most feed.

Redfoot demanded the cleanest ship.

And Redfoot gave the hardest homework.

The crew was unhappy.

"Why do you get to tell us what to do?" clucked one hen.

"How come your nest is bigger than ours?" squawked another.

"And why do I have to do homework if I'm a chicken?" cried a third.

It was a mutiny!

The crew captured Redfoot and made her squawk the plank!

"Wait!" said Redfoot. "I once was free. I clucked. I pecked. I flapped my wings without care. But I wanted MORE than an ordinary chicken life. Now I have more food and treasure than I ever imagined, but everyone is afraid of me."

Redfoot raised her wings,
and tossed her hat into the waves below.

The crew looked at her and clucked to themselves. And then they all threw their pirate clothes overboard.

Together they found a small island to call home.

There they flapped their wings as chickens do.
And Lily gave up the rotten pirate life for good.

But she still had *other* plans.